Words of Color

God's Poetry... *Is* Life...

Missionary...
　　　　William Rice

© 2014 William H. & Jane Rice

Printed By BT Johnson Publishing
www.BTJohnsonPublishing.com
Toll Free 1-866-260-9563
ALL RIGHTS RESERVED

Bio Photo by: Kayla Monté

Printed in the United States of America

Acknowledgements

This may sound strange to some, but others will quickly agree with me. I want to give an acknowledgement, a thank you for all contributions in forming who I am. To everyone, family, friend, or foe, whom I have known either briefly or for long; all have been teachers.

I liken each of you to pies. They're all good, just some are better than others.

But, to the pie, that God baked especially for me, my wife Jane; she is absolutely my most "favoritist", hot or cold, she's it!

So, to everyone I have ever known, or will know, thank you for being a part of the colors and flavors of life!
God loves you!

*Everything in life ...
Is an invitation from God ...*

Our years as a thought ...

A Valid Question to be Answered

Who is this author, and Who is his GOD?

My bio is on the back cover of this book. My God and of Whom I am speaking is:

<u>GOD is *YHVH/ELOHIM</u> - Creator of the universe.

<u>Jesus the Christ – Yeshua ha Messiach</u> – my Savior, the Messiah.

<u>Holy Spirit – Ruach ha Kodesh</u> – the Power and the very Breath of GOD.

Three in One, inseparable, yet separate in function. The Holy Spirit lives in me as my Helper, Comfort, and Counselor; a direct line of conversation with Jesus; so I know the answer to my question, "what is Heaven saying today"?

*Pronounced - YaHoVaH / EL O HeeM
Almighty GOD The Creator

Preface

    These poems have been written from a heart full of emotion. For me, poems are my times of searching. They reveal times of such closeness to God I can hardly breathe, and I must praise and glorify Him. And then, there are the times of "Where are You? Oh, I am the one who moved away?"

    God has a sense of humor and sometimes is even whimsical. He is ever-present, from the most awesome and grand, to the song of a little bird that healed me.

    He has placed color in us and our world to remind us of Him. Colors are His attributes; personality on display; His love for me and you. If this were not true, black and white would do; which provokes the question, "Why even be?"

    And, I just want to share with all of you!

    I hope you enjoy, and find "you"; your words of color and song; joy in the midst of the whirlwind; He is the Eye; my calm.

Color Legend For Poems

Green - Contentment and Peace
Blue - Hopes and Dreams - Faith
Red - Blood and Sacrifice - Precious Love
Purples and Violets - Royalty ... God ...
White - Purity ... Truth and Revelation
Black - Evil and Lostness ...
> *In God's kingdom, the heavens, there is no black...maybe shades of white though. Can we see hell from heaven?*
> *Black in our earthly realm is made up of colors; not a real black.*
> *But, in Satan's realm there is a real black; void of all color.*
> *Colors are for Joy and Contentment; there is none in Hell.*
> *Death may be black but, death of self may bring light and life...*

Yellows and Oranges - Warmth and Comfort

Our lives are all combinations of colors ... hues; shades and values.

Rainbows are visual promises and invitations for life in our God, The Creator. He is reinforcing our knowing in our heart, that He sees and loves to cover us with His beauty.

<u>Words of Color</u>

Words of Color ...
Dispel the black of despair ...

With greens of contentment ...
The blues of hope ...
Black retreats ... there is no need for color in death ...
In the presence of Transparent Red ...

A white in Purity ... surrounds ...
removes all shame ...
Transparent Red now lives ...

Love dispels all black ...
Life given in the truth of His Words of Color ...

Ah ... the light and warm sun ...
Flickering as Breath through the blue leaves ...
The healing whisper ...
The Tree of Life ...

His Words of Color ... fill me ...

Sing Unto The Lord

Sing unto The Lord a new song ...
Praise His name and sing ...
Out of the song of my heart ...
Is my victory ...
His grace and mercy ...

Sing unto The Lord a new song ...
The shadows of evil draw back ...
Unable to stand in the presence ...
Of joy ... song and dance ...
In worship to God All Mighty ...
El Shaddai ...All Sufficient One ...

Sing unto The Lord a new song ...
In praise and worship ...
In thanksgiving is my victory ...
HalleluYah ... where my life belongs ..

Sing unto The Lord a new song ...
Let my life be an instrument ...
Of praise and worship ...
For all peoples to see ...
The drum of thanksgiving ...
The trumpet of praise ...
The cymbals of worship ...
A symphony of love ...

Sing unto The Lord a new song ...
Shout the victory ...
God inhabits my praises ...
My songs of joy ... worship unto Thee.
Love conquers all ...
The shout of praise brings the walls
that march against me ... down ...

Sing unto The Lord a new song ...
The war is not mine ...
The battles are already won ...
I am to stand and sing my new songs
of HalleluYah ...
Thanksgiving ... and Love ...

No Black In A Rainbow

Green is the color of peace ...
Blue the color of dreams ...
Red ... sacrifice ... love ...
White is purity and truth ...
There is no black in a rainbow ...

The Air Is Dark

*The air is dark ...
Crystals of light sparkle bright in the
light of the Son ...*

*The warmth of the crystals fills my
every breath ...
I exhale in blue ... violet ...
purple ...*

*My shroud is green ...
covered in Red ...
As if I am in an ice cocoon ...*

I AM wraps me in Him ...

*The air ...
Is to fullness with brilliance ...
I do not breathe ...
There is no need ...*

His breath is me and I am Him ...

Red Ink

*Who decided red ink is bad ...
And in the black is good ...*

*Maybe God uses red ink ...
To write my name in the
Lamb's Book of Life ...*

*Color me Red ... I am forgiven ...
Black is a lie ...*

What Color Red

What color red did I hear in your words ...
The red of war ... or the Red of forgiveness ...
What color red do you speak ...

Are they blue to violet ... with dreams and hope ...
Given in shades of green to soothe ...
To bring peace ...
White in truth ...
Bright in wise light ...
No darkness in your sight ...

Breathe ...

Death Is Not Their Desire

*In a nation where only the many voices,
In the selfish worship of the mini-gods are heard ...
Unrighteousness and injustice
Is the blood its wolf-pack of judges requires.*

*Death is not their desire ...
But to maim and to tame ...
To make truth of the lie ...*

*That they are the new freedom ...
Security ...
The new name of liberty ...
They have done violence to the law ...*

*The silence of the righteous is to blame ...
Enslaved ...
What shame they have brought upon the Lord's name ...
A love gone cold ... destroys ...*

*Wolves in the temple beware ...
As you stand before your lord ...
Satan says ... well done ...
The blood of dust now covers your shame.*

Do You Love Me

Do you love Me?
Then trust and obey Me.

If you do not trust and obey,
That means you do not believe that
I love you ...

Do you want MY best?
Then give Me all of yours.

Do you want My blessings, My favor,
My grace?
Then give Me all of yours.

Do you want My provision beyond
your needs?
Then give Me all of yours.

Give and do your best,
I will take care of all the rest ...

<u>Love Is ... The Narrow Path</u>

Jesus said to me, piercing through my selfish blind pride,

"Love is ... the narrow path, one drop at a time, one drop wide."

*Lord, "Yes, I see my path it looks as if it has been walked upon?
Oh, yes, one time before, walked by You."*

*You tell me that the path is true,
And that You will bring me through,
I am to always keep my eyes on You.*

*This path so narrow,
So difficult at times,
Where missteps could send me to the place of death.*

*But, You say even in the place of wrong,
You are there to guide me along.*

*You say, "I don't see your wrong, I only see you get back up,
Brush off the dust and move on.*

*When you were down on your knees
and all you could hear,
Was the enemy rejoicing in a
triumphant song,
You tried to close your eyes and ears
to the lies and tears.*

*You cried out to Me and asked,
'Where did I go wrong?'
And you heard Me whisper,
Look down.
You are too weak to hold your head
up, to see My love, to hear My song."*

*As I opened my eyes I could see the
One drop, the path once again.
One drop wide, and the next one,
one drop at a time.*

*Jesus said, "Throw off the load, the
fear that has burdened you down,
collapsed you to the ground.
Lay your life down on the path that is
prepared just for you,
That was walked by Me, one drop at
a time, one drop wide."*

"Yes", He said, "your walk is true,

When We are Two as One; complete.

*Remember ...
When you are in defeat, doubt and
can't see true,
Look down to see,
Is your way intercoursing as one drop
or two,
Separated, at war; with Who?*

Do you see One drop or two?"

The Shear Of Rain

The shear of the rain divides the air,
For some it is despair ...
Yet others say ...
Refreshing ...

The Stain Effected

The stain effected
One step at a time, our time.
One drop given,
One at a time, in His time; to fulfill time.

The stain effected
One step at a time,
On the narrow path We walk together;
One drop of blood wide.

The stain effected
One drop at a time,
On the day one drop of blood was placed in your Mother's womb,
Our Father said, "Good, it is now their time."

The stain effected ...
Cowers at seeing,
Our one drop of blood, given in love, acknowledging our Father's sight.
Covered and cleansed; destroying our plight.

The stain effected,

*One "Yes" at a time,
To give, to hope, to love without fear.
By a narrowed birth in blood and water; a tear.
A foretelling of our path; one drop wide and one drop at a time.*

*The stain effected,
One drop at a time.
But, only the drop sacrificed in our Father's time.*

*One drop at a time,
We add to the love of the ones before that gave their Life blood in His glory.
The stain effected.
One drop at a time.*

Blood Bought Soil

Blood bought soil ...
The fertile ground plowed ...
By men who dared enter the fray ...

To labor in depth to clear the thorns
of evil ...
That tear at men's souls ...

To overcome the ground abandoned ...
With plow in hand ...
And the Sword in the other ...

Planting seed that would be harvested
and in a crucible ground ...
Into the salve that would clean ...
And heal man's wounds ... his soul ...

<u>No Black</u>

*There is no black in Me ...
Are you in Me ... or is that just
something you say ...*

*What color do people see ... in what
you say or do ...
Transparent Red ... or black ...
Me or you ...*

The Light of Darkness

The light of darkness …
Just shadows …
Shadows always deceive …

Step into My Righteousness …
The light brighter than the day …
The light that shows the way …

My light is your life's purpose …
To be the shadow of light …
Truth and love … hope …

A place where shadows of darkness …
May no longer display …

It's Only A Sardine

A fisherman throws his net ...
In a wide circle it is cast ...

He watches the net sink,
He waits in hope for a catch ...

As he pulls in his net ...
His eyes are wide ... for a catch would mean success ...

He springs into action for he sees ...
A fish caught in his net ...

As he untangles the fish from the net with care ...
He holds it up for all to see ...

It is only a sardine ...
But it will do ... celebrate ...

Cool of the Day

Lord, I meet with you in the cool of the day,
Coffee in hand, I sit and I stand, sing and pray.

In Your presence is rest and Your love,
You keep me on course, saying,
"Walk in My steps, My likeness,
Come, this is the way."

To love in My name
Destroys all evil; all evil ways.

Be strong in My heart,
Keep your words true, pure;
To speak from your heart.
The path assigned to you.

My light always prevails,
In thankfulness it assails
The sense of hopelessness,
That no-one cares.

My love, My heart, through My likeness in you

*Shines through the darkness.
When you meet with Me in the cool of
the day,
Coffee in hand wanting to pray.*

Yes, I too, wish you could stay ...

Did I Leave An Open Door

*Lying on my bed in the night, soft and secure ...
Listening to the ocean waves ...
Somehow peaceful in their assault against the shore ...*

*Then I hear a noise next to my bed ...
I turn on the light and sand crabs scurry away ...
Someone had left open a door during the day ...*

*Then I think ...
Oh Lord ...
What door did I leave open today ...*

Don't Go There

Tomorrow is a mirage ...
Yesterday ... shifting sand ...
Today is God's purpose ...

Look for Him in everything ...
If you don't find Him there ...
Don't do it ...
Don't go there ...

Out of the Shadow

*Out of the darkness of my mind
I see a light so pure and true ...*

*Just a glimmer that peeks out through
the shifting thoughts,
Like dust that in their emptiness fill
the room ...*

*The shards of red and green with
blue,
Flash in slow-motion to speak in
boldness
The calming color of I Am with you ...*

*The green brings peace
The blue my smile
All surrounded and covered in red
That says "I've got you ..."*

*The flash of white leaves a smoldering
hope,
A brave dream ... is it true ...*

*A rainbow of breath fills and flashes
Flames of green, yellow and blue,*

With a center of red so warm and pure,
I just want to crawl into You ...

The glimmer is no longer in hide and seek ... it is in full view ...
The dust of my mind blows away when I hear ...
"I Love You" ...

I said, "Where have You been ...
I have been searching so long?" ...
He said, "Right here waiting for you,
Waiting for you to step out of the shadow ...
The shadow of 'you'" ...

Blackness Resumes

In my silence before the Lord ...
He speaks ...
In my thoughts focused on Him ...
He is present ...
If my thoughts wander off of Him ...
My Lord pulls back in silence ...
He will not compete ...
Blackness resumes ...

Something Silent

*So many say, look at our frescos
Look at our marble pillars and floors.
Gilded gold and flashing lights galore,*

*Hear what our leader says
For he proclaims in this palace that
he "knows".*

*All I know is that I came to hear
what Jesus says …*

*Oh … you want me to put something
silent …
In the plate of silver and gold …*

As The Winds Blows

As the winds blow and the water's storm,
The Lord said to me, "Row towards that point," stretching His arm in a direct way ...
I said, "That's against the wind,"
He just looked at me ...

I said, "Yes Sir" and changed my way.

As I rowed against the wind and the waters storm ... I sang praise to my Lord for I know ... He would not point me wrong ...

My arms burned with strain against the storm ... and my eyes stung from the rain ...
I thought, I am so tired, I cannot pull one more stroke ... and the storm is strong ...
Jesus said, "The shore is close, just one more stroke against the rain ...
I know your pain ...
Let Me help with the strain ...
Hey ... we are at the shore ...

We had reached the point ... the sun so bright ...

Breakfast is served in My joy and morning light ...
So ... I sit in love ... with my Friend ...

I see my boat and wonder ...
"How did it make it through the storm" ...
So much damage ... the sails are torn;
I just feel battered and bruised ...
But I am here ... where He told me to be ... so all else doesn't matter ...

I AM loves me ...
and knows where I am ...

The Blood As Dust

Whoever is in apathy ...
And complacency ...
Will hear ... the words of the Lord ...
As bitter ...
Their love...gone cold ...
The Blood as dust ...

Temples

Look at the ancient ruins of marble,
granite and gold,
The morning glory covers
The dust of men ...

The ruins of men ...
Are the temples they build ...
To themselves ...

The Path

*The way of the Father is very narrow
... only through Me.*

*And My way is covered with My
Blood; sacrificed willingly!*

*The path is covered by a single drop
of blood,
Laid down one drop at a time; fully
sacrificed,*

Willingly because of love ...

<u>A Pierced Mind</u>

The world pierces your mind with thorns.
Beats and lashes your back into submission.

Falsely clothes your wounds,
Then rips your covering off to expose,
In humiliation your pain.

If you submit at this point,
You die a slow infected death filled with pain.

If you do not submit
They publically crucify you ...

The Narrow Path

This is the day ...
To trust and obey ...
To sing and to say ...
To laugh and to pray ...
To go in My way! ...
"Jesus, I say yes to Your way!"
"Good", He replies, "Love is the way ...
The narrow path ...
That takes you through the day!" ...

Storms Rage

*Thank you Jesus for today ...
The storms rage in fury outside ...*

*But, with You in me ...
I am content ...*

Silence Now Restrained

*In sparing the rod of discipline ...
In order to not bruise their
self-esteem ...*

*Young men and women, old and
middle ...
Have become nothing stable ...*

*Any idea whether good or wrong,
new or old, that was restrained ...
now in the name of rights and
freedom ... are layers of chaos ...
of fear ... unbound.*

*A voice unrestrained by a rod of
discipline ... shouts for blood ...
All others to blame ...
If they don't conform ...*

*Tyrants ... tyrants ... mini-tyrants ...
all seeking their prey ...
To enslave ... handcuff ... and cage ...
In the name of rights to live their own
way ...*

To push out the God that restrains ...

A godless nation falls prey ... an enslaved nation ... without discipline, handcuffed ... and caged ...

*Led by selfish
Tyrants ... tyrants ... mini-tyrants ...
Have left only one option ...
one way ...*

*To pray to their gods of silver and gold ... wood ... stubble ...
and hay ...*

*In their homes and houses of prayer,
Where discipline stood and kept in silence to the world ...
Silence now restrained ...
Enslaved ... handcuffed ... and caged.*

<u>*The Universe of God I hold*</u>

*I closed my eyes and in the darkness
there were twinkles and sparkles of
light and stars …
they seem so very old …*

*Shooting stars of green … red …
and gold …
I had the whole universe in sight …*

*I am sure the doctors have some long
term for what I saw …
They are so limited in their view …*

*But my universe, my mind's eye …
The universe of God I hold …*

His view is the one to behold …

Butterflies

Yellow ... green ... blue ...
and orange ...
Just passed through my life ...

Butterflies paused in their flight ...
As if to say ... "I see you" ...

Now... What am I to say?

When steel-toed boots and the rifle
butts knock down my door in the
night ... I think ...
"Lord, this is not You" ...

Fear enters in but I hear this small
voice saying ...
"I AM with you" ...

The soldiers drag me outside with
curses, fists, and kicks with their boots
of steel and rifle butts ...

Into the night they throw me around
and then toss me into a cell ... slam ...
click ... all I hear...
"I AM with you" ...

Jesus ... I love You ...
and I sing praises to you ...
These steel-toed boots and rifle butts
are so afraid ...

They think they win if they kill me ...
They don't understand ...
they can't kill me ... I am with You ...

And You are with me ... I have joy ...
They hate me because of You ...

Now Lord ... What am I to say? ...

Old Sign

I saw an old sign made out of a piece
of plywood this morn' ...
It was scarred ... beat-up ...
and torn ...

I looked close and discovered ...
it was four layers of wood ...
Pressed ... formed together as one ...

The Holy Spirit said ...
"This is us in Him ... The Father ...
The Son ... The Holy Spirit ...
and me ...
All held together by the glue of Love
and the Word ...

Be a sign for Me, too" ...

<u>Daddy Loves Me</u>

*This morning I was so sick ...
I asked the Lord to heal me ...*

*He sent a bird to sing me a song
outside my window ...*

*It sang ...
"you are healed ... I love you" ...*

Blue Leaves

*Are people able to rest around you ...
Are you as a tree planted by the river
of Living Water ...*

*Is the shade cast off of you in vivid
blues ... violets ... creams ...
ultramarines ...*

*Are they able to pick a bouquet of
sparkling blue leaves of hope and
dreams ...
Then eat till full with juice running
down their chin ...
In joy ... stick out their blue tongues
and grin ...*

*Is the ground around covered in
greens eight inches thick ...
Or wood, hay and stubble, that prick?*

*Greens of spring and summer ...
So sweet and just the right flavor ...
May they lean against your trunk all
vibrant and pulsing in reds and golds;
Flashing silver in rainbows ...*

*Rubies ... emeralds ... sapphire
marbles with a diamond shooter ...
at ready ...*

*May everyone rest ... sing ...
and play ...
Dance ... run fast ... or kneel and
pray ...*

*Around you ... a place of shelter ...
Or ... are you the storm ...*

Gray Wind

When the winds are gray ... and the
sky is yellow ...
I look for flashes of white ... to strike,
And leave once again a smoldering of
hope ...

Without a fresh blue breath ...
Creating green eyes in me ...
I stand as a crag on the side of a
barren hill ...
Still ... and the color of the wind ...

But ... God in His love for me ...
Fans the fresh Blue Flame to devour
me ...
Creating use out of roots gone dry ...

Silver and gold weave through my
thoughts ...
As blood in a Vine ...

Paper of Black

*My pen writes white on a
transparent paper of black ...
Words suspended in the universe ...
As truth ...
waiting to be breathed in ...
His Word revealed ...
His Breath of Life ...*

Bring To Boil My Blood

As the fires of blue ... violet ... and
green ... rise up in me ...
Bring to boil my blood ...
into purification of truth ...
Pure Spirit of love ...

My words purified in golden red
blood ... refined in green fire ...
Poured over the mist of darkness ...

Bring truth and life of white ... blue
... and green ...
A rainbow ... grounded in His
promise ...

His work requires all of me ...
Only righteous pure blood ...
His covering of me ... will do ...

Every drop will be spent and
delivered ...
As an offering for You ...

Come Forth

*On the battle field I hear the cries of the wounded ...
"Water" ..."Help me" ...*

*Why do I plug my ears and close my eyes ...
To my neighbors' plight ...
to God it is a stench ...*

*Jesus call me forth ...
out of the grave ...
Roll back the stone ...
And unwrap the grave clothes of religion ... traditions ...*

*And "Come Forth" into the Light ...
into life ...
And give His Living Water ...
Hope ...*

Refining

*I close my eyes in worship ...
to my God ...
I see waves of chartreuse green fire ...*

*Refiner's fire of blues and gold ...
orange green ...
Burning the scales and shadows off
my spiritual eyes ...
Like lily pads crossing and
disappearing ... I see blue ...*

*On my left I see the edge of a carved,
scared door ...
But ... I cannot turn to enter in ...
The green fires vaporize
across my view ...*

*I am at a banquet table ... with many
people and food ...
Their plates piled high ...*

*I look at my crystal plate ...
it is empty ...*

*Then I hear ...
"I don't want you to eat at this table,*

I have My food for you"...

*"Wait ...
till the refining is through"...*

Color of Darkness

The shadow of white ...
The color of darkness ...
Is red ... green ... blue ...
Removed ...

The shadow of white ...
The color of darkness ...
Is the Blood of Christ Jesus ...
The green of peace ...
the blue of hope ...
His love ...
Refused ...

Shadow of Pure Love

*Shades of purple ... violet ... and blue,
pulse through my view ...
Surrounded by the transparency of
Red ...
This is Me in you ...*

*The purity of truth ...
and trust you seek ...
The white without shadow ...
Does not exist in you ...*

*Only in Me do you even see the
shadow of pure love ...
An intimacy for eternity ...
Transparency of Truth ...*

I Have You

My eyes are closed to stop the world,
To draw and be closer to You ...

In my mind I see the storm rage ...
The clouds rise up ... the lightning
flash from cloud to cloud ...

Thunder drowning out all sound ...
Trying to cover You ...

I seek harder ...
Fearless to the lightning and thunder,
the winds of storm ...

Then I hear ...
"Relax ... I AM here" ...
"I AM always ... just draw near ...
Without fear or doubt or the rain of
tears ...
Relax ... I AM here ...

I AM the lightning ...
I AM the thunder ...
that breaks through the storm of
clouds and dark ...
I AM the power of thought ...

*Do not focus on the clouds and dark,
I AM the light ...
that destroys the dark ...*

*My thoughts surround you in
protection ... rest ...
I have you ...*

*The reds and blues ... yellows and
greens ... purples ... violets ...
My promise to you ...*

Home With Him

My home in heaven is made with stones of granite, marble, onyx, and lapis, diamonds, emeralds, sapphires, and pearls ...

Every door a red ruby ...

So, as I go into my home and rooms ...
I give thanksgiving, gratitude, praises and worship ...

For only through the Red Blood of Jesus' sacrifice, may I enter in ...
to His joy ...
He builds my home on love ...

My eternal home with Jesus has doors of rubies ... floors of emeralds ... ceilings of sapphires and lapis ... walls of fresh breezes always glowing in His direct light ...
and living water of life ...
There is nothing dead ... no wood furniture ... no cotton underwear ...

A life so vibrant and full ...

*worship to God my Father ...
Pulses through ... my being filled ...
Being home with Him ...*

Breath of a Rainbow

*To breathe in Your rainbow of life
every moment of everyday ...
The blues of hope ... faith ...
and dreams ...*

The greens of peace ... and joy ...

*The reds of love ... the yellows and
oranges of hugs ... warmth ...*

*The transparency of white ... truth ...
The white space ...
between the colors of life ...*

The place of promise fulfilled ...

Reflection

The blindness of selfishness ...
reflects brightly their fear ...
It's all they can see ...

Be My reflection in hope ... faith ...
and charity ... love ...
For all to see ...

I Preserve

*I hear the churches plead ... for help
... help to teach our children ...
our youth ... help clean ...
serve anywhere ...*

*I asked the Lord ... "What's the reason
... what's the problem?" ...
He said ..."Hearts un-changed" ...*

*There are many ways to force service
and obedience ... even the appearance
of loyalty and caring ...*

*But ... love can never be forced ...
or feigned ... un-changed hearts in
forced labor ... soon tire and leave...*

*Leadership that threatens ... are not
of Me ... they are already defeated ...*

*Only a willing ... changed heart ...
filled with My love ... will serve
unselfishly ...
All else is wood ... hay ... and stubble
... made of man ... not by Me ...*

There is rotten fruit ...

*I have reserved a special place ...
for thugs ... tyrants ... and thuggery
disguised as love ...*

Self-less love is all I preserve ...

Cracks In The Concrete

A hard heart is not made of stone ... it is concrete formed ... out of the gravel of lies ... hurts ... the sand of betrayals ... love ripped and torn ... the blood of trust drained by so many wounds ...

A cruel heart is formed ... in fear ... to protect what's left of me ... a misery that cries ... "Help me" ... "Please dare"

I Am the Light that cracks the concrete ... to bring forth the Living Water ... to wash out the gravel ... the sand ... heal the wounds ... My Blood flowing ... now in you ...

Are you willing to share? ... It will cost you ... your blood ... one drop at a time ... your death ...

The death of "you" ...

It's All About Me

*It's all about me ... and my greed ...
is this country's cry ...
What happened to US? ...*

*It's all about me ... and my greed ...
is the church's cry ...
What happened to US? ...*

*We have removed God ... we no longer
include Him ...
We no longer believe ...*

<u>Glorious Is The Moment</u>

*Strikes of Light ...
Waves of Thunder ...
Love is perceived ... delivered ...
A touch in Spirit ... mind ...
yearning soul ...*

*A contentment so violent ...
All else dare not appear ...
To be burned away ...
A pure fire ... prepares the way ...*

*Enter in ... the way prepared ...
Love announced by strikes of Light ...
Waves of Thunder ...
Love perceived ...*

*The Shield of Contentment ...
Destroying the world of chaos ...
Love delivered ...
The touch never removed ...*

*Glorious ... is the moment realized ...
A moment that never moves ...
It is fullness ...
Where would it go ...*

A Train of Thought

A train of thought just went by ...
But ... there was no caboose ...
How will I know the end ...
When it is safe to cross the tracks ...
To safely move on ... hmm...

A Grain of Sand...Stands

The one who stands against the tyranny at hand ...
Stands in the Strength ...
The ranks that number as the sand ...

The evil of tyranny ... home or abroad ...
Rules by fear ...
Terror to make me bow my knee ...

But ... when I stand in the name of Jesus ...
Heaven's Glory and Power braces my knees ...
Knees that will not bend in worship ... sub-mission ...

When I stand ... amongst the terror ... chaos ... blood and gore ...
To their plan of conquest ... submission ...
I bring terror to their hearts ... their chaos ... confusion ... defeat to them ...

Tyranny fears the defiance of Good ...
Resolute Good brings terror ...

To the terror they infuse ...

They do not understand ...
I stand in the promise of God ...the Creator ...
My brothers and sisters are as the number of the sands ...

Sands ...
Stained by the blood of those ...
Who refused to bend their knee ...

I stand on Holy ...
Hallowed ground ...
Grains of sand called by name ...

I Kneel In The Dust

The despair of fear ... the grief that seeks relief ... all before my view ...

Lord ... Your eyes you gave me ... Your ears to hear the cry ... "Who will help me" ... "Does anyone see or hear?" ...

Men who hate ... rule by fear ... destroy by bullet ... sword ... and rape ... strip us naked of all dignity ... and make us surrender ... The hate forces obedience ... my knee to bend ... my face to lower ...

In a whisper ... I speak Your name ... I fill with joy ... my fear and grief relieved ... You hear ... You see ... You are with me ...

I smile and almost laugh ... as I kneel in the dust ... I speak Your name in a whisper ... and frenzy erupts ... I speak Your name again ... then laugh ... the men who hate are in confusion ... running here ... then there ... not knowing what to do ...

*I kneel in the dust ... in reverence ...
and submission to You ... Your peace
absorbing all of me ...*

*I whisper Your name ... and every
ear hears ... I am now in full view ...
Your power of love ... now rules ...*

*The men who hate ... are ruled and
fear You ... they don't know what to
do ...
Their despair of fear ... the grief that
seeks relief ... is all before my view ...*

*Lord ... Your eyes You gave me ...
Your ears to hear the cry ... "Who will
help me?" ... Who will find me? ...
"Does anyone see or hear?" ...
I rise up from the dust ... and stand in
Your power ... and love ...
I raise my hands in praise ...
and shout Your name ...*

The Color of War

Purity ... the color of war ...
A fire so pure in transparent white ...
All impurities of blues ... greens ...
reds ...
The only colors I comprehend ...
extinguished ...

With a flash ...
My knowing is less than a grain of
sand ...
On the beach ...or ...
The bottom of the sea ...

Purity is all I seek ...
Purity ... the color of war ...

I cannot comprehend ...
Transparency ... Victory!

My Champion

The void of darkness ... the deceit of black ...
Is always daring ... challenging in a call ...
To enter into a duel ...

But ... the call of Light ... the absence of all darkness ... or black ...
Dares ... and challenges me ...
To let His Light be my Champion ...
For God says ...
"I am to precious ... I might lose "...

I Am Here

I am here because God loves me ...
I am here ... because one perfect man was dis-obedient to God ...
I am here ... because Noah was obedient to God ...
I am here ... because of Abraham's obedient faith ...
I am here ... because Mary said an obedient ... "Yes" ...
I am here because 12 men said, "Where would we go ... only You have the Words of Life?" ...

I am here ... because one perfect man ... was obedient to God The Father ... Jesus ...
I am here ... because one imperfect man ... me ... was obedient to the Holy Spirit who said ... "God loves you" ...
I am here ... to pass it on ...

My Prayer

My Prayer ...
"For Your glory Father God ...
In the name of Jesus Christ of
Nazareth ... the Name above all
names ...
And by the power of the Holy Spirit,
My Helper ... Comfort ... Counselor ...
Change me ... Change them ...
Remove me ... Remove them ...
Restore me ... Restore them ...
Keep me from evil ... that it may not
harm me ...
Amen!"

Rainbow of People

Who said white is good and black is evil ... and every color in between are just differing degrees ...

God placed a rainbow of color in the sky as a promise of life ...
Life abundantly ...

He also placed a rainbow of people ...
for life ...
Life abundantly ...

Addicted

Some are addicted to bitterness ...
Some are addicted to sweetness ...

Lord ... help me to be addicted to neither ...
Help me to be only addicted to the contentment of You ...

Red Flowers

Green fields covered with trails of red flowers ...
How do I know which trail is mine? ...

Holy Spirit open my eyes ...
That I may see You ...
There is my path ... oh thank you ...
thank you ...

My flower of red that I follow ... one flower at a time ...
It has edges of blue ... pulsing and fading then vibrant and strong ...

Your heart Lord pulses ... drawing me close to follow only You ...
To pursue the path prepared before time ...
In the green fields of contentment ...
Covered in red flowers pulsing in blue,
The trail I leave is a rainbow of life ...
glorifying You ...
For all to see ...
Oh ... thank you ... thank you ...

*I see people in the green fields covered
in red flowers ...
Some are just sitting ... why ...
Oh ... they are refusing to move ...*

*Others are picking bouquets ...
running to this flower and the next ...
just to pick ... to add to their bouquet.*

*Oh ... they're only gathering for
themselves ...
Even taking flowers that are not
theirs ...
Not fully following their path ...
Destroying beauty and the path for
others to follow ...*

*Oh no...their bouquet is wilting ...
Now what do they do ...
They have lost their way ...*

*They can't see the blue of Your
pulsing heart ...
The burst of joy in the center of red
and blue ...
To glorify You ...*

Oh no ... look ... look ... look ...

They are laying down in the black ...
It is growing over them ...
Lord do something ...

"No ... I have done all that I am going
to do ...
I have sent you ...

Look there is a red flower right next
to them ...
Go and show it to them ...
There it is pulsing blue ...

There is always hope ...
If you are willing to go ...
Go into the black ...

Do you see your path ...
It's like a neon road" ...

<u>*I.Q.*</u>

*Wow ... you just cut me off ...
and slammed on your brakes
abruptly ...
I had just passed you ... so, why?*

*Oh ... I see ... you want me to see the
message you have on the rear of your
car ...
The cross ... a fish ... a dove ... oh ...
and the sticker that reads "Jesus
Loves You" ... How thoughtful ...*

*I just noticed you are waving at me ...
You are pointing up ... or ...
Is He number One ...
Oh ... my bad ... now I see ...
It's your I.Q ....*

<u>Did I Miss It...Again</u>

Yesterday does not exist ... anymore,
Only now exists ...

For His purpose ...
To love ... to forgive ... to bless ...
to become one ...

Oh ... Lord ... did I miss it again? ...

Eye To Hear

*Life without color is black ...
despair ...
Rainbows are hope ...
life filling the air ...
For the eye to hear God's love and care ...*

Red Sox

*Am I able to drink the cup that God
has offered me? ...*

*What cup I ask? ...
God smiles in my spirit and says ...
"The very same one I offered to Jesus
In the Garden of Gethsemane ...*

*The cup of life in Me ...
The cup of the death of selfish you ...
The cup of sacrifice to glorify Me ...
And save your brother's life ...*

*The cup of hope ... dreams ... smiles ...
The cup of cool water that answers
their question ...
'Does anyone care' ...*

*Are you the hand that holds out the
cup of loving-kindness ...
Indifferent to the enemy's warning ...
to get away ... let him be ... the kicks
and the shoves ...
To look into the blue-green eyes of
Jesus ...*

*And see loving hope and peace ... in the pain ...
The strength of weakness ...*

*Before you pick-up this cup to use ...
Be sure you read the user's guide ...
Also read the warnings and dangers for improper use ...*

*The cup has already been purchased,
It is free to you ...
But ... the content that fills the cup is not ...
You have to purchase ... pay the price,
Even determine the quality ... quantity ...
Each day you decide to purchase your cup filled with Me ...
Or ... the world ...*

My cup is continually filled ... pressed down ... shaken ... over-flowing in the abundance by and for the Holy Spirit.

*The world's cup ... you have to fill ...
Are you able to drink the cup I offer you ... personally ...*

Choose wisely ... this is for eternity ...

Oh ... you don't know ... you are asking for help ...
You are wise to ask Me ... I AM always willing to help ...

Here is a perfect cup ... especially formed for you ...
There is no other cup like it ...
It matches My heart ... the perfect size and color ... for you ...
It is one of a kind ... just like you ...

There is only one accessory that may be purchased by your "Yes"...

White Sox ...

They will follow the tell ... the footprints I left ...
As you follow the soxs will turn red

Leading you to your Calvary ...

My Corner

*Sheets of gold ...
Oceans of blue ...
Green that invades the scene ...
Flashes of silver and red ...
Nations merge by...determined to arrive ...*

*I Am here on this street corner ...
Stop and say "Hi" ...where ya going?
Oh ... you will know when you arrive.
Oh ... no time for Me ... you need to get going ...*

*The sheets of gold ...
The flashes of silver ...
Are calling you ...*

*Okay ... I'll be right here on My corner ...
Drop Me a line when you have arrived ...*

False gods

*In worshiping false idols ... false gods,
Death is assured ... now ... future ...
eternity ...*

*No hope for life ... now ... future ...
eternity ...*

*False gods require sacrifices of
purity ... innocence ... love ...
death of peace ... rule by fear ...*

*The true God requires protection of
purity ... innocence ... love ...
life in peace ...*

*Giving hope for life ... now ...
future ... eternity ...*

Transparent Oceans

*Transparent oceans deceived
by man ...
In his yellowness of greed ...*

*The depth of a wave ...
The shudder of power ...
Determines the lay of the land ...*

<u>Fear Removed</u>

*Do not dwell on the problems of yesterday ...
That spill into today ...
Peace and contentment destroyed before the dawn ...
Focus ... stay in Me ...
I AM the way ...*

*Trust in Me ...
I AM provision ...*

*Trust in Me ...
I AM all understanding ...
the Victory ...*

*Trust in Me ...
I AM love ... love in Me ... love dispels all fear ...*

*When all fear is removed ...
What is left ...
I AM ... Me and you...
Enjoy the garden I have planted in you ...
Share the harvest ...
In love ...*

I AM ...

<u>Dances of Orange</u>

*The dances of orange ...
The inspiration of blue ...
The fragrance of green ...
Surround you in rings of rainbows ...*

*Please stay on the line ...
I love to talk with you ...*

War Such A Waste

War ... such a waste ...
Stupidity of man ...
Satan's plan realized ... Murder! ...

Tell your wife ... husband ... children,
your brothers and sisters ...
That you love them ...
Show it all the time ...

Do not enter into the argument ...
the combat ...
Where man never wins ...

War ... such a waste ...

In Order To Live

A heart without God is deceived ...
Easily manipulated ...
Tired of the battle ...
Tired of running here ...
No, He's not here ...
Running to there ...
No, He's not there ...

A heart without God gives up with despair ...
Life's not fair ... Does anyone care ...
Where is my hope? ...

A heart filled with God ... Cannot just be still ...
It must give out freely the answer ...
The hope ...
The hope of faith ... the hope of love ...

To set liberty before them ... Freedom
... Courage ...
To live in joy ...
Deception destroyed ...

In the name of Jesus ... Received ...
In order to live ...

A Force Loosed

Wars ... wars ... and rumors of war ...
All started by man ...
Competitions of selfishness ...
These are the ways of man ...

By My hand ... I will end all war ...
My destruction of evil is not ... a gun,
Sword ... bombs ... or suicide
explosions ...

My love is a force loosed ...
By thanksgiving ... praise ... prayer
... and worship to Me ...
First ... going before My Army ...

My love is so complete ...
That evil cannot exist ...
Cleanse yourself ... and come up to Me
Make yourself pure ... in My
Righteousness ... Jesus ...

The Holy Spirit only helps in My
Righteousness ...
Overflowing from your heart ...
Completeness ... you ... Me ...
He never competes ...

We just go ... with thanksgiving ...
praise ... prayer ... and worship ...
Leading Our way ... in declaring
forgiveness ...
Jesus' name ...

Wahoo ... Victory ...

Holy Spirit...Help!...

*So many pastors are in fear ...
Fear to speak with boldness ...
God's Word ...
Holy Spirit ... Help ...*

*Afraid their church board ... or
congregation will fire them ...*

*God is their Boss to Whom they pledge
in covenant ... their life ...
Holy Spirit ... Help ...*

*Maybe I have mis-diagnosed ...
It is not fear ... it is cowardice ...
or ignorance ...
Holy Spirit ... Help ...*

*Afraid to speak the hard word ...
To send out the people ...
To tell about Jesus and His love ...
sin forgiven ...
God is not mad at you ... He wants
you forgiven ...
Or ... do they even know? ...
Holy Spirit ... Help ...*

*Fire the board if they control you ...
Stop holding the hand of the people ...
Saying it is alright ... when it's not ...
Tell them God loves you ...
Holy Spirit ... Help ...*

*Send out the people ... it is what we
all have been called to do ...
The time is now ...
Go and tell ...
The hurting ... fearful ... hopeless ...
enslaved people ...
Holy Spirit ... Help ...*

*Maybe we should turn off the A/C ...
or heat ...
Take the padding off the chairs, pews,
the seats ...*

*So many believers talk a good game ...
Amongst those who believe the same...
Holy Spirit ... Help ...*

*But ... outside the walls of comfort ...
They walk in fear ... Cowardice ...
hurting ... hopeless ...
Enslaved ...
They are just the same ... no
difference ... only in name ...*

Holy Spirit ... Help ...

*I think many accounts in Heaven are almost empty ...
Mansions not even started ...
The style of living undecided ...
Maybe even the neighborhood ...
It is time for some sweat equity ...
Holy Spirit ... Help ...*

*Pastor ... elder ... brother and sister ...
in the pulpit or pew ...
The blame of a godless nation ... evil rampant ... unchecked ...
The blame falls squarely on you ...
Holy Spirit ... Help ...*

*AH ... doesn't that A/C feel good ...
It's so hot out ... I think I'll just sit here today ...
I wonder what's on TV ...*

*More news about ... wars ... famine ... and dis-ease ...
Turn it off ...I don't want to see ...
The hungry ... and homeless ... the thugs in the street ...
The office elected ...*

My pastor says "we should pray" ...

*Maybe I'll just play a video game ...
What the hey ... I deserve time off today ...
Holy Spirit ... Help! ...*

In Consent

Lie ... steal ... kill ... destroy ...
the mantra of satanic rule ...
No regard for life ... the weak of
women ... children ...

To boost their cowardice courage ...
To beat their chests in conquest ...
Give their lives in conscious consent...

The shame is not on them ...
That comes upon believers of Truth ...
Jesus Christ ...
The sacrifice made for me and you ...
them too ...

Our cowardice courage ...
Is to save our lives upon this earth ...
In fear ... to speak ... to be known ...
To give our lives in conscious
consent ...
For our true God to use ...

I AM

I AM ... your everything all the time
I AM ... your love ...
I AM ... your hope ...
I AM ... your faith ...
I AM ... your strength ...
I AM ... your wisdom ...
I AM ... your knowledge ...
I AM ... your thoughts, heart...words
I AM ... steps you take ...
I AM ... your friend who picks you up when you stumble and fall ...
I Am ... the Holy Spirit ... Helper, All

I AM ... you better know it ...
I AM ... real

The Unknown Breath

I saw a man half in and half out of
his smashed pickup truck ...
A wife ... a mother and father ...
or son and daughter ...
To whom he would never come
home ...
When he left his family he expected to
return ...
I hope he said "I love you" ...

What a difference the next unknown
moment brings ...
One breath from eternal life ...
or eternal death ...
Did he know Jesus or not ...

God is in our moments of now ...
In our very present ... not past ...
nor future breath ...

So ... to answer the question ...
so many keep asking ...
"What is Your will God ...
my purpose ... my assignment ...
While I am on this earth?" ...

*The answer is ... with the very breath
of God in you ...
Introduce Jesus to the person in front
of you ...*

Life is your purpose ...

So That I May Continue

Solo-sex ... same sex sex ...
Pornography ...
Vasectomy ... I.U.D ... the pill ...
abortion ...
All are selfish ... selfish me ...

Forgive me, God ... I didn't know ...
I didn't believe ...
I don't believe in You ...

These excuses God refuses ...
Deep ... deep ... down in our
conscience ... we knew ...
All these are wrong ...

Only a seared conscience will disagree
vehemently ...
To reject God's view and purpose for
us ...
Lostness without hope to restore ...

Enjoy ... this life ... It's as good as it
will ever get ... for you ...

We have believed the lies ...
Of pleasure at any price ...

Even at the cost of life ...
So that I may continue ...

There is hope ... forgiveness ... and love ...
Give your sin to Jesus ... accept Him as Savior ...
Then He will direct your way ...

His righteousness ... sets us free ...
and gives us liberty ...
From selfish me ... to give me life ...
So that I may continue ...

The Crumbs

The land is black ...
The sky a deep-night blue ...
It is the midnight hour ...

I see faint particles ... as if on a table top ...
Then a hand sweeps across the black land ...
It is sweeping the faint crumbs from the table ...
into His other hand ...

As He sweeps ... the crumbs glow ...
Like burning phosphorous ... in a rainbow of color ...
Explosions ... flares ...

Everywhere else the land is black ...
The sky a deep-night blue ...
Waiting for your hand in God's ...
To sweep in the crumbs ...
Celebration of salvation ... rockets ...

A Heart Issue

*Your eye is the gateway to your heart
... to your mind ... your ear ...
Guard what you see ...*

*Turn your eye away from evil ...
vulgarity ...
No evil or vulgarity are you allowed
to speak or think ...*

*You have a heart issue if you do ...
Take care of it ... then return to Me ...*

My purity ... not naivety ...

*My revelation ... understanding ...
wisdom ... discernment ... help ...
And gifts of the Spirit ...
Only come in My purity ... in you ...*

<u>The Light of God</u>

The Light of God ... Shows in the death of you ...
My Light shines when you put you ... aside ...

Throw off the filthy rags ...
Be washed in My Blood ... so that I Am may clothe you ... in Me ...

All people then see ...
My Light of brilliance in you ... I Am glorified ... you lifted up ...

I draw all men by My Light ...
Draw 360 and all will see ... every facet of Me in you ...
Any darkness ... will be exposed ...
Destroy it ... before it destroys you ...

What does Light have to do with darkness ...
Nothing ...

Revolting Development

*Today I took more time to shave and
comb my hair than I did to pray ...*

*Isn't that a revolting development ...
Yep ...
That pretty much sums up my day ...*

Be Counted

*As I hear ... and see the thunder ...
lightning ... the fallout of rain ...
I hear the battle rage in the heavens...
The roar is about me ... to obtain ...*

*The battle is fierce ... both sides in
total array ... fully committed ...
To the point that only death ... would
be their pay ...*

*The Commander of the Heavenly
Host ... has won the war ...
Set the prisoners free ... you and me...*

*But ... the battle still rages ...
The enemy still roams the land ...*

*The Commander calls ... to all who
believe ... His good ... His cause ...
To stand ... to be counted ... to stand
in your place of order ...*

*Your purpose is true ... our
assignments ... carried by His Word...
In you and me ...*

Out of the Ashes

Out of the ashes I rise! ...
It is the life I lose that brings life! ...
I will follow! ...
Help my faith ... my joy! ...

Fearful Godless Men

Fearful godless men are starting to rule ... men whose only aim is to win ... not for the good of all ...

To win regardless of truth ... or cost ... loss on their part not an option ... lie ... steal ... destroy ... the opposition ... truth not in them ...

They do not assign the Pledge of Allegiance to the United States ... to themselves ...

"I pledge allegiance to the flag of the United States of America ... to the Republic for which it stands ... one nation under God ... with liberty and justice for all" ...

*These are not words or virtues that have meaning for them ...
Godless government ... and mean-spirited men ...the destruction of US...*

They may enslave ...the populace ... but ... they also build their graves ...

*and tombs ... of eternal torment ...
and fear ...
fruit to eat ... thereof ...*

The Stone I Send

*My heart spoke a truth in the empty chaos of my mind,
In the earliness of day,
Of a love unknown but sought,
The Truth, the Love, whispered out of the fray,
"Stand still and know Me, My peace."*

*I Am your day, the only way through the fray.
A hope, a faith resolved, so you may say, "I am okay."*

*"What makes you so special?" so many say,
"I've been bought by a price paid,
Out of love, and a hope, a faith with absolute resolve,
That I would say, 'Yes' to a better way."*

*Beloved, hold fast to Me and My way,
For the cowardice of chaos screams fear,
Their demise, defeat, the mirrors shattered in My light.*

*The time is now for the rocks to be known,
For the rocks to be thrown,
At the glass and mirrored houses there contain,
False thrones.*

*You are the stone that cries out,
My truth, My love, showing the way.
Stand still in the chaos as a stone,
Anchored to the Rock;
The altar, thrones contained in glass and mirrored houses distained,
And fear the most.*

*Your silence in peace speaks loud amongst the chaos,
Boldly in courage whispers hope and love, a faith resolved,
Attracts all who say, "What makes you so different this day?"*

*You are the stone that cries out,
The stone I send to be; My way ...*

Light Of His Name

When the light returns,
The shadows will burn away ...

When the Sons of God stand up ...
All nature will rejoice and
All sickness and disease will
Be destroyed in the fire of the light ...

No shadows can remain, in the
Light of His name ...

My God, the God of Renewal,
Who sees me turn and return to Him,
everyday ...
Who cleanses me in the fire of His
light ...
And rejoices when His love in us
withstands the test ...

When, I was a toddler He helped me
walk ...
But, when I became a man He wept ...
For I thought I could stand on my
own ...

*As my shadows grew darker ... to where I could not stand ...
I stumbled and fell ...*

*He called to me and said,
"Remember ... I am your God, the Father, the Daddy of Renewal ...
Turn towards the light ... return to Me." ...*

*Then the shadows will burn away ...
And no shadows can remain ...
When I walk in His name ... Jesus! ...*

Ah - A Breath

As a man enters into His intimacy,
It is familiar and yet new ...

A touch, a stroke, a scent,
Ah - A Breath ...

The place that is Promise,
The place that is Hope ...

The remix of tomorrows,
Yesterdays and yet, today ...

There is just the hint of mystery,
A familiar touch that catches a breath ...

A breath of intimacy, closer ...

Cross the threshold ...
Close the door ...
Enter in - you are safe ...
Do not hold your breath ...
For I have said, "Yes." ...

The Promise given ...
The man accepted ...
The Hope that is real ...

The touch, the stroke,
The scent, ah – the Breath ...

Renewal ... the familiar yesterday!
In excitement ...
I have no thoughts for tomorrow ...
Or yesterday ...

Now is the touch ...
Now is the stroke ...
Now is the scent ...
Ah – the breath is now ...
Enter into the promise that is real ...

A man enters into His intimacy
It is familiar and yet new ...
Now is so pleasant ...
At peace safe and secure ...

The Promise fulfilled ...
A man accepted ...
In the Hope that is real ...

Now is real ... all else pales ...
The touch ... the stroke ... the scent ...
Ah – the Breath ...

All else a mystery to unveil ...

Tomorrow

Tomorrow is yet to form ...
Yesterday has passed away ...
Today is now ...
Lord in you ... let it be! ...
Amen.

A Promise To Be

*Yesterday ... just an aroma of a
shadow ... of a thought ...
Today ... the sweet smell of a new
birth ... with the energy ...
of bright eyes ...
Tomorrow ... just a vapor ...
a promise to be ... maybe ...*

There Lays The Problem

*Lord ... I need Your help ...to resolve
the lies ... manipulations ... deceptions
words of blood ... pen ... and hurt ...*

*The enemy accuses and reminds me of
my sins daily ... by moments of
weakness ... when I want to be strong,
a mountain of sin burdens and buries
me ... weighs me down ...
I cannot stand ... the accuser is loud.*

*Thank You, Holy Spirit ... I hear You,
You say ... Hallelujah ... Bring them
on ... I will deal with them one by one,
ready ...*

*Oh ... Lord ... will I survive this ...
He said ..."No" ... Do you believe Me ..
I said ..."Yes ...
as completely as I know how" ...
He said ..."There lays the problem ...
as you know how" ...*

*Now ... in Me ... go and sin no more,
Only in Me do you live in
righteousness ...*

*When the temptations of lust for the
flesh ... pride ... superiority ...
criticism ... arise ...
I will tell you "No" ... stay in Me ...
We will go through this ... In humility
Removing the mountain ...
into the sea ...
All chains broken ...
The strength that destroys the enemy.*

Wahoo ... shout the Victory! ...

What Color

I look at my hand ...
I see not just one ... but two ...
Your hand on mine ...
or is mine on Yours ...
No matter we are pulsing as two then one ...
Me and You ...

Lay hands on the sick ... the infirmed, the lost ...
Speak restoration ... health ...
sins forgiven ...
I love you ...
Take up your bed and walk ... your color and joy ... returned ...

What color is healing and Love ...
Look at your hand ...
What color are you ...

One Way

My way ... or there's the highway ...
My way ... is the narrow way ...
Love ...
You follow Me ... In single file ...
One way ... One Voice ... One Word ...

Grace

*Grace sees the good in me ...
Through Jesus Who hung on the tree...*

*God's grace so amazing ...
For all the world to see ...
Even when I give You no reason to
love me ... You say, "come closer" ...*

*In Your grace I have liberty ...
The only chains on me ...
Are the ones I choose to wear ...*

*Help me to understand ...
It's not about me ...*

Isn't This Fun

In the auditorium of my thoughts ...
I heard a wall crash down ...
Surrounded now in the blast of dust
and debris ...
The Lord says ...
"Wait I want you to see ...
Just wait in Me ...
It is My pleasure to reveal ...
Trust Me ...

Isn't this fun ...

The Gift

*The Gift is true that comes from You
It is a part of what I am to do.*

*To be thankful and enter into Your presence,
Such a gratitude of praise.*

*To use this gift for all to see,
Makes You smile, rejoice and say,
"Oh, how he honors Me."*

*To value this gift and share,
Shows you care for all that I love.*

*The true gift of love is the hardest one to receive,
And even harder to share.*

*But, it is the only one that says "you care for Me."
Love is most difficult to believe.*

*Please receive the most precious gift of My love,
In faith and hope in Me.*

Then share this love with all you see,
In this loving-kindness so rare.

You will be a beacon that draws men to Me,
For they, too, long to receive My true gift of love
In faith and hope; belief in Me.

The light on the hill is My true gift of love,
Shining out of you for all to see.

Even a smoldering reed in a place of darkness may be seen,
Accept fully My gift of love and then I will fan it to flame.

The true gift of My love is what all men seek,
This gift of loving-kindness so rare.

Share everywhere, you have plenty to spare,
I gave you all that you could bear.

The gift of love was bought by Me on Calvary

At the highest price that only I could pay.

Yes, the gift love is true that comes from Me,
It is all that you are to do!

<u>Just a Random Thought ...</u>

*It doesn't make sense ...
To not be doing what you love ...*

The gift you have ...
Give back to Me ...

Prayer

*Father God, in the name of Jesus
Christ, and by the power of the Holy
Spirit who lives in me ...
I want Your Life fulfilling me ...*

*You are my Savior ... my Strong
tower ... my ever-present Help ...
Thank You for your Grace that calls
me "The Apple of Your Eye".*

*Form me into a sweet apple pie ...
A sweet aroma to You and all those
around me ...
The savory flavors of You ...*

*Open my heart ... to Your heart ...
Open my eyes ... to Your eyes ...
Open my ears ... to Your ears ...
Holy Spirit ... help me to open my
mouth and speak with courage ...
the Words of Color!
Amen...*

An Impartation of the Aaronic Blessing

'Y' varek'ha *YHVH v'yishmerekha
(May YHVH bless you and keep you)

Ya'er YHVH panav eleikha vichunekka
(May YHVH make His face shine on you and show you His favor)

Yissa YHVH panav eleikha v'yasem l'kha shalom
(May YHVH lift up His face toward you and give you peace)

So I shall have the YHVH's name on my forehead, and He will bless me.
Numbers 6:22-27

Seek His intimacy, discernment, revelation, understanding, wisdom, and help. He has blessed you and me! Peace and blessings are ours to walk in ... so by faith we do!

*Pronouned - YaHoVaH - Almighty GOD The Creator

Other Books By William Rice

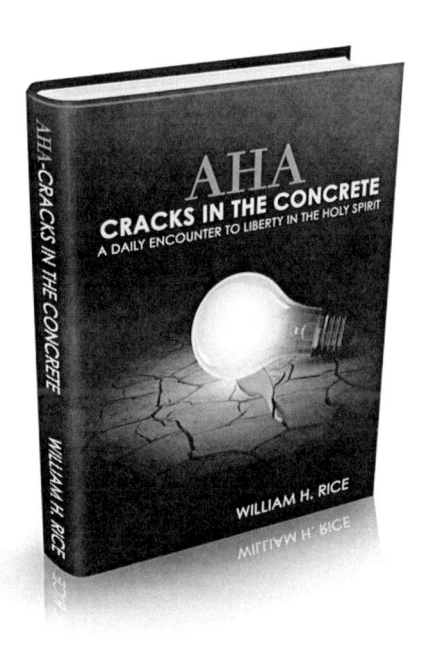

AHA-Cracks In The Concrete
A Daily Encounter To Liberty In The Holy Spirit

The contents of this book may be hazardous to your thoughts...
your relationship with god and family...
present health...
your mind...
your life...
Life has a purpose!

Marriage can be difficult, but it doesn't have to be. God created marriage to be a powerful force of unity. Unfortunately, we sometimes destroy this unity by strife, contention; selfishness.

A "happy marriage" is not just a concept. It can be a living reality.

We have 100's and 100's of marriages and relationships that shouldn't be; <u>but they are!</u>
They are thriving and happy because they chose to Argue Naked.
Stop fighting, and start uniting today.

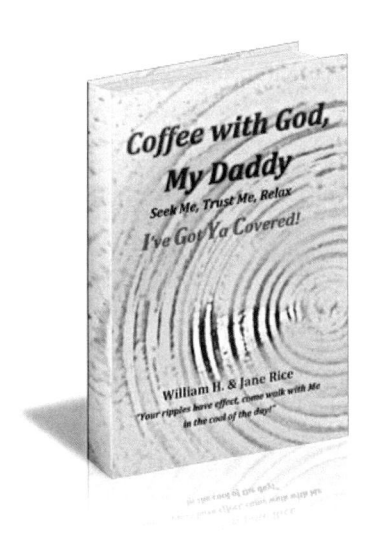

"It was like I was reading the Psalms. As I began to read, <u>Coffee With God, My Daddy</u>, I was struck by the stark transparency of this Godly man's intimate time with the Lord. I found myself completely drawn into his experience, such transparency of his heart, in times of difficulty. I am requiring all my leaders to read this."

Dr. Terry Knighten, Founder and Senior Pastor, Renew Church, New Braunfels, Texas

Start your day in His presence, with a cup of coffee and His Word. When you are in unity with God, seeking, putting Him first (Matthew 6:33), you are absolutely able to believe and know,

"Seek Me, Trust Me, Relax, I've got ya covered!"

By the Bible...
or By the Bayonet...

When did we lose sight and stop working for the common good of all men and the communities that make up our nation? When did religious and government control combined with corporate profits become a priority over the welfare of people? When did we forget the very foundation this country was built on, a unifying belief in God's promises? When did we forget that we are able to do something about it? When did we forget God and His power in our lives?

We are a like-minded force of ordinary people, unified by the Holy Spirit, to be the Good News; the very heart of God.

For the Kingdom of God is not just a lot of talk; it is living by God's power. (1Corinthians 4:20 NLT)

"Be fit in your faith, fearless!"

Contact William and Jane Rice

Revivedn2@gmail.com

Whether we are rich or poor, if we do not have peace and health, we have nothing of full life value; our life is shortened.

Jesus as our Savior is life at its fullest.